JIM FROG

For Ferd Monjo R.H.

For Diane M.B.

Text copyright © 1983 by Russell Hoban
Illustrations copyright © 1983 by Martin Baynton
All rights reserved, including the right to reproduce this
book or portions thereof in any form.
First published in the United States in 1984 by
Holt, Rinehart and Winston, 383 Madison Avenue,
New York, New York 10017.

Originally published in Great Britain by Walker Books Ltd.

Library of Congress Cataloging in Publication Data

Hoban, Russell.
Jim Frog.

Summary: Jim Frog feels a little low in the morning,
but by evening he decides it hasn't been such a bad
day after all.
[1. Frogs—Fiction] I. Baynton, Martin, ill.
II. Title.
PZ7.H637Ji   1984   [E]   83-12586

ISBN: 0-03-069501-5

First American Edition

Printed in Italy
1 3 5 7 9 10 8 6 4 2

ISBN 0-03-069501-5

JIM FROG

RUSSELL HOBAN

Illustrated by
MARTIN BAYNTON

HOLT, RINEHART AND WINSTON
NEW YORK

Jim Frog was feeling a little low,
a little lonely, he had no hop in him,
he just dragged himself along.

At chorus practice he wouldn't sit up
straight on his lily pad, he just flopped
around. When everyone else croaked
'Jug-of-rum' he croaked 'Mug-of-jum.'

'Stop that!' everyone shouted. 'Why
can't you croak 'Jug-of-rum' like the
rest of us?'

'Nobody likes me,' said Jim.
'Everybody hates me.'

When it was snack time everybody else got their nets and went out to catch dragonflies. Jim couldn't be bothered, he wasn't hungry, he couldn't find his net, he didn't care. He took his harmonica out of his pocket and played sad songs.

A head came out of the water, it was Big John Turkle, the snapper.

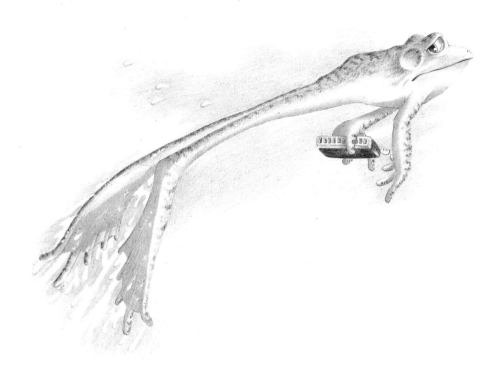

When Jim saw Big John
he hopped away fast.
'Nobody likes me,' said Big
John Turkle. 'Everybody hates me.

Jim swam down to the other end of the pond. He stuck his head up through the duckweed and saw a damselfly nymph crawling slowly up a cattail stem.

'Go ahead,' said the nymph. 'Eat me, I don't care.'

'I'm not hungry,' said Jim.

'Everything's been so utterly rotten,' said the nymph.

'I've been feeling a little low too,' said Jim.

'Everything seems to be closing in
on me,' said the nymph. 'I can scarcely
breathe, I feel as if I'm going to jump
out of my skin.'

'I feel a little lonely,' said Jim.

He was looking away from the damselfly
nymph when he said that. When he looked
back he saw her empty skin split right down
the back and the damselfly was out of it.

She looked altogether different. She
waved her new wings dry and then she flew
away, blue and glittering, across the pond.

'How did she do that?' said Jim.
'I wonder if I can do it?' He climbed
onto a lily pad and tried to jump out of
his skin but his skin jumped with him.

'Ladies and gentlemen,' said a voice,
'your attention, please: Roland Waters
the pond-famous diving beetle will now
dive from a height of one inch into two
feet of water.'

The voice belonged to Roland
himself. 'Drumroll, please,' he said to
the cicada who was his partner.

The cicada did the drumroll and
Roland dived into the water.

'Did you see that?' he said to Jim. 'What a feat!'

'I thought it was two feet,' said Jim.

'What a joker you are,' said Roland. 'But it really was something, wasn't it? I think everyone was impressed.'

Jim looked all around but he couldn't see anyone but the cicada, who was dozing in the sun.

'I suppose so,' said Jim.

He felt like being alone so he went
down to the bottom of the pond and swam
into a hollow log. He took his harmonica
out of his pocket and began to play it.

Big John Turkle looked in. The hole
in the log was too narrow for him
so Jim was safe there.

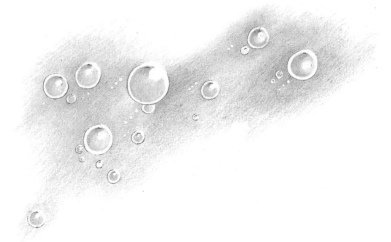

'I can see the bubbles but I can't
hear any music,' said Big John.
    'Neither can I,' said Jim, 'but I
know what I'm playing.'
    'Is it happy or sad?' asked Big John.
    'Sad,' said Jim
    'That's funny,' said Big John, 'the
bubbles look happy.'

Jim went home. He noticed that he had a lot of hop in him. He thought of Roland Waters and he began to laugh. He was laughing and hopping, laughing and hopping, all the way home.

When he got home his mother said, 'You look as if you've been having a pretty good day.'

'Actually it hasn't been bad,' said Jim, 'not bad at all.'